# The Ancient Storehouse of Jedi Wisdom!

In his dream, Luke saw himself on a secret mission in the rain forest.

When he looked up, he saw a circular wall made of blocks of green marble. In the center of the circle was a tubular transport for descending underground.

Luke dreamed that he could see his Jedi Master, Obi-Wan Kenobi, standing at the wall, beckoning him, signaling Luke with a wave of his hand to come closer and enter.

"Luke," said Obi-Wan, "this is the entrance that leads underground to the Lost City of the Jedi. The entire history of the galaxy and all its worlds is recorded there, protected by the caretaker droids of the city. Your destiny is linked to one who lives down there."

THE LOST CITY OF THE JEDI

STAR WARS®

The Adventure Continues...

Book 2

# THE LOST CITY OF THE JEDI

## PAUL DAVIDS
## AND HOLLACE DAVIDS

Illustrated by Karl Kesel

A BANTAM SKYLARK BOOK®
NEW YORK • TORONTO • LONDON • SYDNEY • AUCKLAND

RL 4, 008–012

*THE LOST CITY OF THE JEDI*
*A Bantam Skylark Book/July 1992*

ISBN 0-553-15888-0

Published simultaneously in the United States and Canada

Bantam Books are published by Bantam Books, a division of Bantam
Doubleday Dell Publishing Group, Inc. Its trademark, consisting of the
words "Bantam Books" and the portrayal of a rooster, is Registered in U.S.
Patent and Trademark Office and in other countries. Marca Registrada.
Bantam Books, 666 Fifth Avenue, New York, New York 10103.

PRINTED IN THE UNITED STATES OF AMERICA

CWO    0  9  8  7  6  5  4  3  2

To our parents,
Cecelia and Frank Goodman,
and Frances and Jules Davids,
May Yoda's wisdom grace you always…

# Acknowledgments

With thanks to George Lucas, the creator of Star Wars, to Lucy Wilson for her devoted guidance, to Charles Kochman for his unfailing insight, and to West End Games for their wonderful Star Wars sourcebooks—also to Betsy Gould, Judy Gitenstein, Peter Miller, and Richard A. Rosen for their advice and help.

# The Rebel Alliance

Luke Skywalker

Princess Leia

Han Solo

HC-100

Ken

Chip

Dee-Jay (DJ-88)

Baji

# The Empire

Trioculus

Grand Moff Hissa

Emdee-Five (MD-5)

Grand Moff Dunhausen

High Prophet Jedgar

Commodore Zuggs

Supreme Prophet Kadann

Triclops

A long time ago,
in a galaxy
far, far away...

# The Adventure Continues . . .

It was an era of darkness, a time when the evil Empire ruled the galaxy. Fear and terror spread across every planet and moon as the Empire tried to crush all who resisted—but still the Rebel Alliance survived.

The Rebel Alliance was formed by heroic men, women, and aliens, united against the Empire in their valiant fight to restore freedom and justice to the galaxy.

Luke Skywalker joined the Alliance after his uncle purchased a pair of droids known as See-Threepio (C-3PO) and Artoo-Detoo (R2-D2). The droids were on a mission to save the beautiful Princess Leia. Leia, an Alliance leader, was a captive of the Empire.

In his quest to save Princess Leia, Luke was assisted by Han Solo, the dashing pilot of the spaceship *Millennium Falcon,* and Han's copilot, Chewbacca, a hairy alien known as a Wookiee.

Han and Luke eventually succeeded in rescuing the Rebel Princess, but their struggle against the Empire did not end there. Luke and his ragtag group of Rebel freedom fighters battled armor-clad stormtroopers and mile-long star destroyers. Finally they destroyed two of the Empire's mightiest weapons:

the Imperial Death Stars, which were as big as moons, and powerful enough to explode entire planets.

In the course of his adventures Luke sought out the wise old hermit, Obi-Wan Kenobi, who became one of Luke's teachers in the ways of the Jedi Knights.

The Jedi Knights, an ancient society of brave and noble warriors, were the protectors of the Old Republic in the days before the Empire was formed. The Jedi believed that victory comes not just from physical strength but from a mysterious power called the Force.

The Force lies hidden deep within all things. It has two sides: one side that can be used for good, the other the Dark Side, a power of absolute evil.

After the deaths of the two evil Imperial leaders—Darth Vader and Emperor Palpatine—a three-eyed tyrant who claimed to be the Emperor's son rose to lead the Empire. However, he was a liar and an impostor. His name was Trioculus. Trioculus was aided in his rise to power by the Central Committee of Grand Moffs, a group of sinister Imperial governors who spread terror, misery, and fear on many planets. Grand Moff Hissa had masterminded the secret plot to put Trioculus on the throne, as part of an even darker plot that would give the grand moffs more authority.

However, Kadann, the Supreme Prophet of the Dark Side, foretold that the rightful heir to the Emperor's command would wear the glove of Darth

Vader, a powerful and indestructible symbol of evil. To strengthen his claim to be Emperor, and to unite the Imperial warlords who had been feuding among themselves, Trioculus embarked on a search for the glove.

Despite Luke Skywalker's efforts to prevent Trioculus from ever finding the glove of Darth Vader, Trioculus recovered the prize on a mission to the ocean world of Calamari. There the Imperials and the Rebels survived a deadly undersea explosion, leaving their fates unknown to one another.

Trioculus is now on a journey to see Kadann, to seek the Supreme Prophet's dark blessing and acceptance of his claim to be the rightful ruler of the Empire.

Meanwhile, Luke has arrived in Cloud City on Rebel Alliance business, and he is now on his way to visit Han Solo before he returns to Alliance headquarters on the fourth moon of Yavin.

Unknown to Luke, a strange dream is about to lead him on a mysterious quest— a search to find the legendary Lost City of the Jedi!

# CHAPTER 1
## The Bomb and the Dream

As Luke Skywalker knocked on the door of Han Solo's warehouse, a lens popped out of the metal wall, making a curious noise as it examined Luke's face.

*BJEE-DITZZZ! BJEE-DITZZZ!*

"Please show your galactic ID card and stick out your hand for a fingerprint check," an electronic voice called out.

"Gracious," exclaimed See-Threepio, Luke's golden droid. "Han has certainly become strict about security!"

Artoo-Detoo whistled timidly in agreement.

"Maybe that's because Han's warehouse is in Port Town," replied Luke. "This happens to be one of the most dangerous neighborhoods in Cloud City— a hangout for all types of alien hoods and sleazy, small-time gamblers."

Luke stuck his left hand into the slot, since his right hand was artificial and didn't have any fingerprints. It was mechanical, a replacement for his real right hand, which he lost in a lightsaber duel with the evil Darth Vader.

*ZHOOOOOM!* The door made a loud sound as it lifted up, allowing Luke and his droids to enter the warehouse.

Chewbacca, the Wookiee, greeted Luke with a friendly squeeze. "Rooow-rowf," he growled.

"Easy there, Chewie, not too hard," said Luke. "I've got a bruised shoulder."

Luke, Threepio, and Artoo had come to the planet Bespin on a mission for SPIN—the Senate Planetary Intelligence Network. Lando Calrissian, the governor of Cloud City, had requested their help because food pirates had invaded all of the big hotels and food storage companies. In the raids stolen food was shipped off to a secret Imperial base for the Empire, who needed food for its army of stormtroopers.

Artoo-Detoo had helped design a Warning and Detection Device—a WADD—to protect the food warehouses. It was an infinitely more sophisticated security system than the old, somewhat primitive device that protected Han's rented warehouse. Luke and his droids had just finished installing a network of delicate WADD units, and since they were in the neighborhood, they decided to drop in on Han.

"ChNOOOOg-bzeeep," tooted Artoo to Chewbacca. "KROOOpch shbeeek znooob pvOOOM!"

"Artoo would like to point out," Threepio translated, "that Master Luke's shoulder was bruised when we helped the Cloud Police capture a gang of Imperial food pirates—all of them on Cloud City's *Most Wanted* List. One of those nasty rogues kicked Master Luke in the shoulder, causing the skin tissue to turn blue and black."

"We usually refer to it as black and blue," Luke put in, as he rubbed his sore shoulder. "Hey, you ol'

Wookiee," he said, turning to Chewbacca, "are you taking good care of my friend Han?"

"Graaawrrr," roared Chewbacca, indicating that Han was being well cared for.

"Hey, kiddo," said Han, peeking out from underneath his unfinished house, his hands filled with tools. The house was floating in the air, about three feet above the warehouse floor. Han dusted himself off and stepped out to greet his friend. "How's Her Royal Highness, Princess Leia?"

"She misses you," Luke said.

"She does?" Han asked with a hint of excitement in his voice. "I thought she was so mad at me for going off to build my sky house, that she'd have forgotten me by now."

Luke shook his head. "She misses you quite a lot, in fact. When you said good-bye to leave for the Kessel mission, she. . ." Luke stopped himself in midsentence, glancing around in sudden amazement. "Wow! I didn't know that you were building a mansion, Han."

"A floating mansion," Han said, laughing.

Han took Luke on a little walk around the outside of the house, pointing out all of its special features.

"I've been from one end of this galaxy to the other," said Han, his voice swelling with pride, "and I've never seen another house like this one. It's a new concept of mine—houses that float in the sky. If you don't like the cloud you're living on, you just drift off to another one."

"Rowww-Roofff!" growled Chewbacca. The

Wookiee turned a repulsorlift control knob, causing the house to lower smoothly and gently to the floor.

"Chewie wants to show off the floor plan, so step right inside," Han said.

Luke couldn't believe his eyes. Han's house had outdoor observation decks, a big kitchen under a transparent dome, lots of bedrooms with floating beds, a circular living room that could be turned to face any direction, a workroom for building everything from blasters to airspeeders, a two–cloud-car garage, and—

"Impressed?" Han asked with a wide grin.

Luke smiled and nodded.

"Very impressive," said Threepio. "What do you think, Artoo?"

"Chziiiich!" Artoo tooted enthusiastically, indicating that he was very impressed indeed.

"I was just wondering, Han," said Luke, "is there any special reason why you made the house with so many bedrooms?"

"Why do you ask?" Han replied suspiciously.

Luke gave a shy smile. "Well, I guess I was just wondering if you ever intend to get married and fill this house with kids."

Han laughed. "Who, me? Give up my bachelor ways and settle down? That's a real long shot, if ever I heard one." Han scratched his chin, giving Luke's question a little thought. "Of course," he went on, "I suppose I'd have to admit that there's always one chance in a hundred that it could happen."

Luke looked his old friend straight in the eye.

"Come on, Han," he said, "you can tell me. Were you thinking about marrying my sister Leia when you built this huge place?"

Han just laughed. "If I ever do decide to get married, which is *highly* improbable, Leia is at the top of my list. But this is all just wild speculation."

"Very wild speculation, I'm sure," Luke said, nodding. But the truth was, he wasn't so sure.

Han changed the subject by putting on a chef's apron and cooking them a spicy Corellian meal on his new nanowave stove. The hot and saucy dish was a favorite back on Han's home planet. Chewie then demonstrated his newfound cooking abilities by serving up one of his zoochberry pies for dessert.

"Congratulations, Chewie," Luke said, patting his full belly when they were done eating. "That was about the best zoochberry pie I've ever had! I wish we could stay longer, but we've got to return to Yavin Four now and get back to SPIN headquarters."

Han and Chewie accompanied Luke, Threepio, and Artoo to the hangar where Luke had parked his Y-wing starfighter spaceship. "Are you sure I can't talk you into coming back to Yavin Four with me?" Luke asked Han. "SPIN could sure use your help."

"I'll pass," Han replied. "All I want to do now is complete *my* mission—which is finishing my sky house."

The two buddies said their farewells, and after the two droids were aboard, Luke shut the door to his Y-wing starfighter. He strapped himself into the pilot's seat, waiting long enough for Han and Chewbacca to move a safe distance away from the ship.

Luke pressed the power button, only nothing happened except—

*KLIK-KLIK-KLIK . . .*

The clicking sound kept growing louder and louder. Luke leaned forward to check the switch.

"Careful, Master Luke," Threepio said, "that sound might mean that—"

But before Threepio could finish his sentence, a sudden explosion hurled Luke back in his chair, so hard that his safety straps tore loose.

*BROOOOMMPF!*

Luke flipped over backward, knocking his head against the floor. The blast hurled the thruster into his right arm, tearing open his mechanical hand.

The interior of the spaceship was in shambles. Flames were spreading, filling the ship with smoke.

Within seconds, Han and Chewbacca burst in-

side to help. Chewbacca and Threepio quickly put out the fire, and Han lifted the thruster, freeing Luke's trapped hand. Then he knelt beside his friend.

"You seem to be in pretty bad shape, kiddo," Han said. "We'd better get you some medical attention."

"Oh, I do hope you'll be okay, Master Luke," said Threepio. "One of the food pirates obviously sent us a nasty farewell present."

"Grrooooof!" moaned Chewbacca, holding up a tiny, charred mechanism he found on the floor.

"*Dweeeep dzeeen-boop!*" Artoo tooted.

"Yes, yes, Artoo, I know," Threepio replied. "That's a miniature bomb detonator. Manufactured by the Empire!"

Thanks to the help of Lando Calrissian, Luke was transported at once to the Cloud City hospital, where a team of medical droids examined him immediately. The news about his condition was encouraging. Luke had lots of bruises and several cracked ribs, but no broken bones. However, the control unit in his mechanical right hand had been smashed by the spaceship's power booster.

Luke couldn't bend the fingers of his mechanical hand at all. And the hospital didn't have the right spare parts. In fact, not a single medical supply outfit in Cloud City had them. Luke's artificial hand would have to be repaired back on Yavin Four, and delicate surgery was definitely required.

It was obvious to Han that Luke was going to need a pilot and a spaceship to get him back to Yavin's fourth moon. It might take weeks to repair Luke's Y-wing starfighter, and besides, Luke was in no condition to pilot. Han resigned himself that his sky house was going to have to wait. Friendship came first.

With Chewbacca serving as Han's copilot, they departed with Luke and the droids at dawn. The *Millennium Falcon*'s hyperdrive unit was in tip-top condition. At faster-than-light speed, it was the quickest trip Han had ever made from Cloud City to the fourth moon of Yavin. As they made their approach, the moon loomed before them in space, wrapped in the green glow of its luxurious forests.

When Luke awoke from a long nap, Chewbacca was already shutting down the hyperdrive thrusters, and See-Threepio and Artoo-Detoo were preparing for the landing.

The *Millennium Falcon* began a smooth descent toward the main landing bay of Yavin Four. There they were met by Princess Leia.

"Don't worry, your Highness," Han said in a reassuring voice, as Leia led them toward the Senate building. "Luke had a little run-in with an exploding bomb, but fortunately your brother's like a Kowakian lizard-monkey that has nine lives."

"Thanks for bringing him home," Leia said.

"Hey, what are friends for?" Han said, putting an arm around her. He stared deeply into her bright, brown eyes. "Luke said you missed me," he said. "Sorry I've been such a hermit, Princess. I'll make it up to you. I promise."

Han stopped Leia to give her a very long kiss.

And against the Princess's better judgment, she didn't try to make it any shorter.

While Luke lay in bed in the Central Clinic of Yavin Four, recovering from the operation that repaired his mechanical hand, Princess Leia asked his permission to send Threepio and Artoo to the neighboring town of Vornez.

"I want them to examine and help upgrade a new group of protocol droids that arrived from the planet Tatooine," she explained. "The new droids can't speak as many languages as Threepio, and they've never been programmed to translate the beeps of an Artoo unit, either."

"I guess I can survive without Threepio and Artoo for a week or two," he said.

A few days later, when Luke had almost completely recovered, he went home from the Central Clinic to his private hideaway on Yavin Four—a white stone tower, built long ago by a vanished alien race called the Massasi. On this foliage-covered moon, many of the ancient archaeological wonders of the Massasi still stood, reminders of these ancient people and their society.

Luke's bedroom was at the top of the tower, just beneath the turret. Standing by one of the windows, he admired the sweeping view that overlooked the neverending rain forest. As dusk became nightfall, Luke lay on his bed and stared up at the stars. Before he knew it, he was sound asleep.

Soon Luke's sleep became fitful.

In his dream, Luke saw himself on a secret mission, zooming along on his airspeeder. He was close above the treetops of the rain forest—and then suddenly the forest burst into flames, with smoke rising all around him. Luke was coughing, choking, losing control of his airspeeder.

It tumbled down into the burning foliage. Luke fell off, plunging through the vines and thick leaves. He landed with a thud on the forest floor. When he looked up, he saw a circular wall made of blocks of green marble. In the center of the circle was a tubular transport for descending underground.

Luke dreamed that he could see his Jedi Master, Obi-Wan Kenobi, standing at the wall, beckoning him, signaling Luke with a wave of his hand to come closer and enter.

"Luke," said Obi-Wan, "this is the entrance that

leads underground to the Lost City of the Jedi. The entire history of the galaxy and all its worlds is recorded there, protected by the caretaker droids of the city. Your destiny is linked to one who lives down there.

"Memorize this code, Luke," Obi-Wan continued. "Its importance shall soon become clear to you: JE-99-DI-88-FOR-00-CE." Then he began to fade away.

Gasping, Luke suddenly awoke from his dream. Beads of sweat dripped from his forehead. He still felt some pain from his ribs.

It was early morning. Luke climbed out of bed, walked over to the narrow tower window, and looked down at the treetops of the rain forest. He wondered what his dream meant. Since the day when Obi-Wan Kenobi had been cut down by Darth Vader's lightsaber blade, the Jedi Master had appeared to Luke several times in visions. At the moment of his death, Obi-Wan's body had mysteriously vanished, leaving the physical universe for a world unknown.

Obi-Wan Kenobi was a Master of the Force, but now Luke could feel the Force inside himself.

He dressed quickly, walked down the tower stairs, and climbed into his airspeeder.

Soon he was soaring above the rain forest, just like in his dream, thinking about Obi-Wan Kenobi's mysterious words.

Luke flew the airspeeder faster and faster.

He didn't understand why. He didn't know where he was headed.

He just trusted the Force—and kept going.

# CHAPTER 2
## Ken's Secret Journey

Ken was sound asleep when his pet mooka leapt onto his bed and licked his face, trying to wake him. It was like this *every* morning. When would his mooka learn that boys didn't like to get out of bed in the morning? Especially twelve-year-old boys like Ken who always went to bed late.

"Kshhhhhhhh," the mooka cried. "Kshhhhhhhh."

"Down, Zeebo," Ken said, pushing his mooka away. "Get down. How many times do I have to tell you not to bounce onto my bed in the morning. Do you think I like your feathers getting all over my pillows?"

"Kshhhhhhhh."

"And stop kshhhhhing in my ear," Ken added. "You do that every morning too. Just once I wish I could hear the bark of a dog, or the meow of cat, instead of the kshhhhh of a mooka."

Zeebo made a whining sound.

"Oh, c'mon, Zeebo—I didn't mean it." Ken pet his mooka behind one of its four pointy ears. "Don't be jealous. You know I love you. Besides, I've never even seen a cat or a dog—except in pictures in the Jedi Library."

Ken got out of bed and stood on tiptoe to reach his

computer notebook, which had a small data screen designed to help write essays and organize his assignments. Ken kept it behind some supplies on his highest shelf, hidden away so that his Homework Correction Droid, HC-100, wouldn't find it if he came snooping around.

HC-100 resembled a droid Ken had studied about called See-Threepio, a golden, human-shaped droid that belonged to the Jedi Knight Luke Skywalker.

DJ-88, the ancient, very knowledgeable droid who was the caretaker of the library, had custom-designed HC-100 for the specific purpose of correcting and grading Ken's homework assignments.

Ken examined his computer notebook, pressing the keypad to call up a report he was working on called "The Moons of Yavin."

When the words flashed on the data screen, a number flashed up, too: "65."

After the number was the comment: "You can do better than this, Ken. Suggestion: Add more detail about moons one and two."

"Oh no!" exclaimed Ken. "This isn't fair at all, Zeebo. HC obviously snuck into my dome-house, found my computer notebook, and graded my report, even though I didn't even finish it yet! He gave me a 65; that's practically failing! HC is turning into a spy and a nuisance and—and I won't miss him a *bit* when I leave today on my secret journey Topworld."

"Kshhhhhhh. . ." Zeebo whined, jumping into Ken's arms and licking his face affectionately.

"Of course I'll miss you," Ken said. "And I know

you'll miss me. Chip and Dee-Jay would probably miss me, too, if droids could have real feelings."

Ken considered Chip, short for Microchip, his best and only friend. Ken often wished that Chip were a human boy, rather than just a metallic droid who was programmed to act like a boy and keep Ken company.

Dee-Jay, Ken's nickname for his caretaker, DJ-88, was a droid that Ken deeply admired. But Ken didn't really consider Dee-Jay a friend, since he was also his one and only professor. Dee-Jay taught Ken astronomy, ecology, computers, and about fifteen other subjects.

"In a way, Zeebo," Ken said, "it was thanks to Dee-Jay that I finally discovered the code to make the tubular transport leave here and go Topworld. Of course Dee-Jay doesn't know that I know it. I peeked into one of his files—a file he told me was none of my business. I know it was wrong. But I've been waiting all my life to take a journey Topworld, and none of the droids will let me. Just think what it will be like—getting to see the rain forests of Yavin Four, riding a starfighter with the Alliance, and maybe even—"

Suddenly, without even a knock, the door to Ken's dome-house popped open, and Chip hurried in carrying a tube of vaporizing tooth-cleaner and a canister of foam soap.

"A very pleasant wake up to you, Ken," said the boy-shaped silver droid, who had flexible, ribbed arms and legs that could bend in almost any direction. "I see that you've hardly even begun to get ready to go to the library for your lessons with Dee-Jay. I'll have to stop trusting the mooka to wake you up on time."

Ken took the hint and began to get dressed. He took off his silver pajamas and then put on his silver school clothes. He didn't know why, but silver was his favorite color. Maybe it was because of the semitransparent, silvery crystal he always wore around his neck. Or maybe it was because silver was the color of Chip. And Chip had been his droid friend and helper for as long as he could remember.

Chip's clumsy boot-shaped feet clattered as he stepped over to the trickle of water flowing down the back wall. The hot, natural water never stopped flowing into Ken's dome-house. It came from an underground stream, and he used it to wash up every morning.

The boy-droid, who was about the same height as Ken, picked up a bowl and began to fill it.

"You should have vapor-cleaned your teeth and combed your hair half an hour ago!" Chip exclaimed.

Ken ran his fingers through his moppy, light-brown hair. "I happen to like my hair when it's messy," Ken explained. "And I don't think a twelve-year-old boy needs help vapor-cleaning his teeth. Do you?"

"Master Ken, you know very well that I don't think. I follow my program. And my program is quite strict. Wake Ken. Wash Ken. Feed Ken. Tell HC whether or not you've done your homework. And speaking of homework, look out the window, Ken!"

Ken didn't have to look out the window to know

that HC was about to enter through the rounded, arched front door. HC had very distinct footsteps, like a soldier marching, and Ken could always hear him coming from the rhythmic sound of his metallic feet.

Sure enough, HC entered Ken's dome-house, his bright blue metallic eyes taking everything in, and his round, open mouth looking as if he had just been caught by surprise. As soon as HC began talking, he sounded like a sergeant in the Rebel Alliance army.

"Time for homework corrections!"   HC-100 declared. "And I certainly hope you've given more attention to your other assignments than you did to your report on the moons of Yavin."

"I wasn't even finished with that report, yet, HC!" Ken protested. "And you snuck in here and graded it already!"

"Excuses, excuses," replied HC. "It looked finished to me!"

"Well it wasn't," Ken insisted. "For your information, I was planning on adding stuff about moons one and two. I wish you'd stop coming into my dome-house when I'm not here and grading my computer notebook before I'm ready."

"You know the rules," said HC. "I'm allowed in here for a surprise homework-check at any time."

HC immediately went over to Ken's desk and found the notebook he was looking for.

"Let's see, for Jedi philosophy you've written an essay on the Force. Well, that's a very worthwhile subject to write an essay about," HC said, nodding his head enthusiastically. "And I see that you've finished your quiz on the history of the Great War against the Empire. You've learned to spell Emperor Palpatine's name correctly. He certainly was a horrible emperor, no doubt about it. The galaxy is better off now that he's dead. And what have we here—hmmmmmm, you've correctly described Darth Vader's role as Emperor Palpatine's second-in-command, but, oh no, you've made a serious mistake in your quiz on the Rebel Alliance. Luke Skywalker didn't pilot the *Millennium Falcon* in the first battle against the Death Star. It was Han Solo, and Chewbacca was his copilot. I thought you knew that, Ken!"

Ken sighed. "I do. I guess I must have been daydreaming."

"Daydreaming?" HC asked, surprised. "About what?"

Ken wondered how much to tell HC about his daydreams. He thought about it, as he slowly ran his forefinger across the crystal he wore around his neck. It was shaped like half a sphere, veined with deep blue lines and attached to a thin, silver chain. Ken had worn that crystal as long as he could remember, since the days before he had been brought to this underground place as a very young child. Ken didn't know who had given it to him. And if any of the droids knew, none of them had ever been willing to answer any questions about it.

"I guess I was daydreaming about actually meeting Luke Skywalker and Han Solo and Chewbacca," Ken said finally. "I wonder what it would be like.

Imagine, flying off with them in the *Millennium Falcon!*"

"Honestly, Master Ken, you worry me sometimes," HC said, shaking his head. "Imagine, a boy of your age, wanting to go gallivanting around the galaxy with the Alliance! Remember what Dee-Jay told you. Down here where we live, there's no evil. But up there, Topworld, the spies of the Empire are everywhere, and the Dark Side is strong!"

"I'm not afraid of the Dark Side," Ken said, as he finished getting dressed. "I'm old enough to go Topworld. I want to find out for myself what the real world is like."

"Nonsense."

While HC continued going through Ken's school files, Chip turned on the vaporizing tooth-cleaner and stuck the tip of it into Ken's mouth. "You'll be old enough to find out about the real world when Dee-Jay says you're old enough, and not a day sooner!" Chip exclaimed. "Never forget that it's the duty of us droids to take care of you and make sure no harm ever comes to you. You're a very important boy! Aren't I right, HC?"

"Indeed," HC agreed.

Ken yanked the vaporizing tooth-cleaner out of his mouth. "What makes me so important?"

"Well, for one thing, because *we* raised you," HC replied. "It isn't just *any* boy who can say he was raised by caretaker droids of the Jedi Knights. And we've allowed you to learn many Jedi secrets, I might add! Why do you think we treat you like royalty here? Like a prince—a Jedi Prince."

"Personally, I don't think *real* princes have to put up with getting tooth-cleaner pushed into their mouths every morning by some droid. And real princes have banquets, they don't just drink vitamin syrup for breakfast, lunch, and dinner."

"My, how you exaggerate," Chip said.

HC, meanwhile, continued to grade Ken's homework.

"How did I get to be with you droids anyway?" Ken asked. "And when will you tell me who my parents are?"

"Dee-Jay is the only one who is programmed to answer those questions, Master Ken. And he promised to tell you when it's time for you to know."

"But when will that be?"

"No one knows but Dee-Jay."

"And that's the way it should be," HC added, without pausing to look up.

"Dee-Jay likes to keep secrets," Ken said. "He probably won't tell me until I'm as old as Commander Luke Skywalker; or maybe not even until I'm two hundred and seven, like—"

"Chewbacca is two hundred and five," HC interrupted.

Chip put the vaporizing tooth-cleaner into Ken's mouth once again, and Ken promptly took it out.

"Did you ever stop to think that I might be tired of being cared for and protected all the time?" Ken demanded. "Especially by droids."

"I've told you a thousand times, Master Ken, I don't think," Chip said. "You certainly should know that by now."

"And I don't think, either," HC added. "I merely evaluate and process information—and give grades, of course. Fortunately, one doesn't have to be able to think in order to give grades."

Ken hopped back into his bed and positioned his pillow under his head. "Well maybe if you droids could think, it would occur to you that I'd like to have some friends who are my own age."

"Why, Master Ken, I was manufactured the same month you were born," Chip replied. "I *am* your own age."

"I meant a *human* friend. Not a robot—not a, a droid."

"Please, Master Ken. You must stop thinking about these things until it's time," Chip said. "And now is the time to wash your face, clean your ears, and drink some vitamin syrup. You've got to hurry off to the Jedi Library. Dee-Jay is waiting for you to begin your lessons."

"My ears and my face are clean. And I'm not hungry," Ken said. "And that's final. Good-bye, you two!"

Ken gave his mooka a quick scratch behind the ears. He then picked up his computer notebook and stepped out of his dome-house, *pretending* that he was heading straight for the library.

He walked along the rocky path, looking around at the huge underground cavern. Ken knew that this might be the last time he would see his home for a very long time.

As he looked around, he saw domes of all sizes, lit up by a soothing glow from bubble lights and fluorescent rocks. There were travel tubes, computer cubes, and droids of every imaginable size and shape, all going about their programmed business.

The droids were always busy—modifying the computers, making new droids, repairing old droids, working the power generators, and cleaning and maintaining the hundreds of domes throughout the city. Occasionally they even went Topworld for supplies, and to update the history of the galaxy for the Jedi Library.

When Ken reached the place where the path divided, instead of turning toward the Jedi Library, he stepped briskly toward the tubular transport shaft that went up to the surface of Yavin Four. The low-pitched whine of the shaft was almost drowned out by the loud thump of his excited heartbeat.

Ken opened his computer notebook and took out the metal key-card he had secretly made in Droid Repair Class. The key-card was the same size and shape as the one Dee-Jay always used to activate the tubular transport. Ken now had his own key-card, punched with all the correct code numbers. But would it work?

The glowing, round tubular transport was ready to make its journey straight up, through miles of Yavin Four moonrock. And Ken was ready to make the journey Topworld, to a world he had only read about in books, and seen in pictures and holograms.

He clenched his teeth and inserted his home-made key-card into the slot.

*VWOOOOP!*

The tubular-transport door slid open, inviting him to step inside. This was the moment Ken had been waiting for!

Suddenly he heard the clatter of metal feet approaching him from behind. "Ken, this is *very* irregular!" a familiar voice cried out.

Ken glanced over his shoulder—it was Chip!

"It's *worse* than irregular," Chip continued. "It's forbidden. You know full well you're not permitted to enter the tubular transport and go Topworld until you're a man. Besides, you didn't take your vitamin syrup. How do you expect to ever become big enough and strong enough to defend yourself?"

"But I hate the taste of vitamin syrup," Ken protested. "I want to find out what real food tastes like for once in my life. I want to have some dessert for a change. And I don't mean vitamin mints, either—I mean *real* desserts, like ordinary kids get to have. I want to see the sky, and the rain forest. I want to travel to other stars and planets."

"What would Dee-Jay say about this if he found out?" Chip interrupted in a very annoyed tone. "*I'll* tell you what he'd say. He'd say I neglected my duty and let you run off where you could be killed by Imperial stormtroopers, or eaten by wild beasts, or—"

"Chip, I'm going Topworld," Ken said insistently. "And don't try to stop me. But as long as you're here, you might as well come along. I may need a droid to help me."

*DWEEP-DWEEP!*

The tubular transport started beeping—a signal for all passengers to enter.

"You don't know what you'll find up there in the Topworld!" Chip said in a panic-stricken voice. "What do you know about bounty hunters, or, or—" Chip stammered, "or stormtroopers, or Imperial grand moffs, or Mynock bats, or Rancor creatures. There are alien boy-sellers who might steal a boy like you and sell you into a life of slavery in the spice mines of Kessel!"

Ken ignored Chip, and grabbed the silver droid by the arm, tugging him into the tubular transport. Suddenly the door slid shut. Ken pushed the button that said TOPWORLD, and the tubular transport began to rise like a rocket.

*PHWOOOOOSH!*

Higher and higher it zoomed. Ken stared out the

window. Faint lights seemed to be dancing out of the blackness, like sparks of colored fire. It was the glow of luminous rocks.

"Relax, Chip," Ken said. "This will be fun."

"Fun, Master Ken?" Chip said. "Droids aren't programmed to have fun. You should know that by now."

"Believe me, I do," Ken said in a disappointed voice.

Suddenly Ken felt as if his stomach were flying away from him. The tubular transport was going so fast it seemed almost out of control.

Ken and Chip each held tightly onto the hand-rails with all of their strength. "Oh, mercy," Chip said. "I was never designed to take the trip Topworld."

Ken shut his eyes and held his breath. And then, when he had held his breath as long as he possibly could, the tubular transport finally began to slow down, and then it stopped.

*DZZZZZT!*

The door slid open, and Ken took his first cautious steps into the rain forest.

In front of them was a beautiful wall of bright green marble. Together they went through an opening in the wall; the soft green light of the rain forest dazzled Ken's eyes.

Ken had a faint memory of having seen this rain forest before. Perhaps it was when he had been a very small child, on that fateful day that the droids had only hinted to him about, when the Jedi Master in the brown robe had carried him down to the safety of the city built by ancient Jedi Knights. There the Jedi Master had left Ken, with no reminders of his past, nothing except the crystal he wore on the silver chain around his neck. Ken didn't even have a hologram photo to remember what his mother and father looked like.

Ken continued to walk forward, leading Chip through the thickets of trees and vines, without knowing where they were going. Ken's ears welcomed the sounds of the jungle—the cawing and chirping that filled the air like a song. It wasn't long before they completely lost track of where they were and how to get back to the round stone wall of the tubular transport!

# CHAPTER 3
## Flying with the Force

As Trioculus's Imperial strike cruiser plunged through deep space, Grand Moff Hissa sighed with relief. It was good to be hurtling through space again. They were safe now.

Hissa's pulse quickened as he recalled the narrow escape he and Trioculus had made from the Whaladon-hunting submarine back on Calamari. They had escaped just moments before the gigantic underwater explosion caused by Luke Skywalker.

Now they were on their way to the Null Zone to see Kadann, the Supreme Prophet of the Dark Side. And three-eyed Trioculus, who had declared himself to be the new ruler of the Empire, proudly wore the glove he had found during their undersea journey—the glove of Darth Vader.

Grand Moff Dunhausen, Hissa's most-trusted commander, came hurrying over, his earrings jangling and shaking. Dunhausen always wore earrings shaped like little laserblasters.

As Dunhausen informed Hissa of a dismaying message that had just been received, Hissa bit his lip and lowered his head. Hissa would have liked to have had good news to bring to Trioculus, but it seemed good news was in short supply.

Grand Moff Hissa found Trioculus inside the ruler's private quarters aboard the strike cruiser.

"My Dark Lordship," Grand Moff Hissa began, "Grand Admiral Grunger still refuses to accept your claim to be Emperor—that is until Kadann, as Supreme Prophet of the Dark Side, officially gives you his dark blessing. In that case, Grunger will withdraw his objections and will order his fleet of starfighters to follow your command."

Trioculus gritted his teeth. "And what is his excuse for withholding his loyalty?"

"Like so many of the others, my Lordship, he doubts your claim to be the son of Emperor Palpatine."

Trioculus snarled in anger. "What about COMPNOR?" he hissed in a low growl. "Has COMPNOR replied to my demand for loyalty?"

COMPNOR was the Commission for the Preservation of the New Order—a group of powerful, brutal Imperial terrorists.

"My Lordship, COMPNOR also waits to serve you until you receive the dark blessing of Kadann."

Trioculus furiously blinked all three of his eyes—his two ordinary ones, plus his third eye, which was perched in the middle of his forehead. "What more does that black-bearded dwarf want?" Trioculus stormed. "He made a prophecy that the new Emperor would wear the glove of Darth Vader, and I have found the glove—that should be enough for him!"

"Kadann may be a dwarf, but I suggest that you don't underestimate him, my Lordship," Grand Moff

Hissa offered. "Before he will give you his dark blessing, he has to examine the glove himself to make sure it's really Darth Vader's. I suggest you respect him—and be wary of him. He's crafty and sly. Expect him to try to trick you. And to test you."

With his right hand—the very hand that wore the glove of Darth Vader—Trioculus gripped a round control knob on the navigation panel.

"One other thing about Kadann, sir," Grand Moff Hissa added. "It's important that you speak the truth to him, no matter what he asks you. No one has ever deceived the Supreme Prophet of the Dark Side and lived to tell about it."

Trioculus frowned, squeezing the control knob even harder, as if he were choking a disobedient stormtrooper. The beacon at the top of his Imperial strike cruiser turned on. It sent out an intense light, sweeping across the blackness of space in search of his destination—Space Station Scardia, home of the Prophets of the Dark Side.

Luke Skywalker was just above the top of the rain forest on Yavin Four, speeding faster than his airspeeder was designed to go. Luke squinted against the onrushing wind, racing madly without giving any thought to where he was going. It was as if someone else were the real pilot of his airspeeder—as though he were being pulled by a power greater than his own.

When he looked down, the tops of the trees blended together into a streak of blurry green. The only landmarks on the horizon were the tops of the ancient pyramids.

But Luke was soon out of sight of the pyramids, lost and alone in the sky, with no understanding of where he was headed or why. Then he saw a stone sticking up very slightly above the treetops.

He slowed down his airspeeder, hovering and circling the stone.

He could see that it was like a steeple, perched at the top of a small temple hidden among the trees—a temple built by the ancient Massasi tribe of Yavin Four.

Luke piloted his airspeeder to a landing, breaking through the thick blanket of leaves at the treetops. At last he was on soft ground, near the base of the ancient temple. The floor of the rain forest was dark. The foliage was so thick the skylight couldn't shine through.

Luke felt the pull again. The Force was guiding him, drawing him to walk past the tangle of twisting vines and radiant flowers that were in front of him.

A voice inside Luke, however, told him he should go back. His conscience was telling him that Princess Leia, Han Solo, and Chewbacca would be worried about him.

But for the moment Luke followed a different voice instead. It was a quiet voice that made scarcely a sound. It was the inner voice of the Force, a voice that only a Jedi Knight could hear.

Luke left his airspeeder near the base of the temple and walked through the thick foliage.

He heard someone speak in rhyme, and he stopped cautiously in his tracks.

> *"You come from afar*
> *So very welcome you are."*

A strange alien humanoid with green, rubbery skin was leaning over, digging up a purple flower. When the alien stood erect, Luke could see that he was almost nine feet tall. Instead of hair, there were short, snakelike vines growing out of the top of his head.

The alien glanced at Luke and spoke again:

*"Baji is my name*
*I'm glad that you came."*

Luke's experience in life had taught him never to be too trusting. He put one hand on his lightsaber, unsure whether Baji was a friend, or an enemy pretending to be a friend.

"What are you doing here, Baji?" Luke asked.

*"A Ho'Din healer am I*
*May these plants never die*
*From them comes health*
*The only true wealth."*

Baji held up the purple flower just beneath Luke's nose. Luke cautiously took his hand away from his lightsaber and touched the flower. He took in its sweet, strong fragrance.

Baji explained:

*"A Ho'Din healer never lies*
*Kibo plants cure the eyes*
*So rare and hard to find*
*For the blind man, so very kind."*

Suddenly Luke noticed a silvery gleam of light shining from behind a shrub. It was something made of metal, and it was moving.

Could it be a weapon?

Luke leapt to his feet, drew out his lightsaber, and turned on its power. It was now a deadly, glowing sword, ready for battle.

"Come out from behind there, whoever you are!" Luke said.

There was the sound of crinkling leaves. Whoever was hiding in the brush was trying to crouch and keep out of sight.

"Show yourself," Luke said. "This is your last warning!"

A silver, boy-shaped droid instantly popped up from behind the bush. "This is highly irregular!" the droid exclaimed. "Do you always threaten innocent droids who are merely taking a walk in the forest?"

"Why are you spying on us?" Luke asked. "Who are you?"

"I'm not programmed to give out my name to strangers," the silver droid said.

"That's just what I'd expect a spy to say," Luke replied.

A boy who seemed to be about twelve or thirteen poked his head up alongside the droid. "Don't blame Chip," the boy said. "I was the one who said we should come here. But I'm warning you, if you're a soldier of the evil Empire, you'll never take me alive!"

Luke grinned. "I'm not an Imperial soldier," he said. "I've probably fought more Imperial stormtroopers than you can count. What's your name?"

"Ken," he replied.

"Ken what?"

The boy shrugged. "Just Ken. I was never given a last name by the droids."

"What droids?" Luke asked suspiciously.

"Chip, and the droids who live near my dome-house, of course," Ken said, touching the silvery crystal he wore around his neck. Then he squinted and looked Luke in the eye. "Do you always ask strangers so many questions?"

Ken brushed the leaves and thorns off his clothes and stepped out from behind the branches. Chip, whose feet were tangled in a vine, struggled to get free of the twisted plant.

"Here, let me help," Luke offered.

*FWOOP!*

With one quick stroke of his lightsaber, Luke cut the vine between Chip's feet, setting the droid free. Then Luke returned the lightsaber to his belt.

"Thank you," Chip said. "That's much better. But just in case you were wondering, I was about to get untangled all by myself."

"And now we'd appreciate it if you'd tell us *your* names," Ken said.

Baji spoke first:

> *"Baji is my name*
> *From the planet Moltok I came."*

"And I'm Commander Skywalker," Luke volun-

teered, "Jedi Knight and Alliance pilot, from Tatooine."

Ken's mouth fell open in shock, his sparkling blue eyes gleaming with wonder.

He dropped down on one knee and bowed his head, as if he were a serf who expected to be knighted by a great king. "Commander Luke Skywalker," he said, "I can't believe it. I thought it was you, but I said to myself no, it couldn't be. This is the greatest honor of my life!"

"You've heard of me, then?" Luke said.

"Heard of you! I've studied you! I know almost everything you've ever done!"

Luke smiled and put his hands on his hips. "Really now? I don't think even *I* remember everything

I've ever done."

"Yoda was your Jedi Master!" Ken said. "And before you met Yoda, you learned about the Force from Obi-Wan Kenobi! And you saved your sister, Princess Leia, from Darth Vader, who was really your own father, who turned to the Dark Side when—"

Now it was Luke's mouth that fell open in shock. Who *was* this boy?

"This is *highly* irregular," Chip interrupted. "Why just this morning, HC was correcting Ken's homework, and Ken seemed to know almost *nothing* about you, Commander Skywalker. He thought *you* were the pilot of the *Millennium Falcon,* instead of Han Solo. But now that he's run away from our underground home, he suddenly thinks he knows *everything* and doesn't need his droid teachers anymore."

"Why have you run away from home?" Luke asked.

"You'd run away from home, too, if your only friends were droids."

Puzzled, Luke knitted his brows and put a hand on Ken's shoulder. "The home that you ran away from, Ken—is it an underground city that was built long ago by Jedi Knights?"

But before Ken could answer, they heard a crunching noise in the forest. It was the sound of approaching footsteps.

Baji stepped back cautiously as Luke reached for his lightsaber again. Suddenly a very large and powerful-looking droid pushed aside some branches and walked toward them.

The droid's body was white, and his radiant red eyes shone like rubies. His strong, dignified metal face even had a metal beard.

"Dee-Jay!" Ken exclaimed. "What are *you* doing here?" He was so surprised, he accidently dropped his computer notebook to the ground.

"You have a great deal of explaining to do, young man!" Dee-Jay scolded. "The rules were made to protect you, to keep you safe until you are old enough."

The towering, white droid then turned to Chip. "And you, Chip," Dee-Jay continued. "You've broken my trust."

"I did my best to talk him out of coming Topworld," Chip explained timidly. "But he's a disobedient boy, with a head as hard as stone. He never takes orders, you know."

"I'd be happy to take orders from Commander Skywalker," Ken said. He glanced at the last of the Jedi Knights. "Commander Skywalker, I want to sign up with the Alliance. Will you take me with you? I want to fly in starfighters, and fight the Empire, and—"

Before Ken could say anything more, and before Luke could reply, Dee-Jay raised his hands, releasing a foggy white smoke from his fingertips.

*FWISHSHSHSH!*

The smoke spread instantly, creating a thick, blinding mist.

Luke coughed as he breathed the white smoke and fanned the air with his hands. Rubbing his eyes, he strained to see. But he was enveloped in the misty cloud.

Luke called out for Ken. But when the mist began

to clear, Ken, Chip, and Dee-Jay were gone.

"I've got to find Ken!" Luke exclaimed. He was convinced that Ken could show him how to find the Lost City of the Jedi that Obi-Wan Kenobi had spoken about in his dream. Luke now understood why the Force had led him to this spot.

Baji turned to Luke and spoke discouraging words:

> "Jedi Knight
>   Your search is in vain
> Gone they are
>   Deep into the forest of rain."

But Luke was determined to try to find out where they had gone. He began looking for a trail, for some hint of their path.

It wasn't until Luke was out of sight that Baji discovered the computer notebook that Ken had dropped on the ground. He opened it. On the inside cover, the boy had written:

This notebook belongs to Ken
Dome-house 12
South Jedi Lane

# CHAPTER 4
## The Dark Blessing

"Approaching the Null Zone, your Lordship," said Imperial Commodore Zuggs, the beady-eyed, bald officer who was piloting Trioculus's Imperial strike cruiser.

"Keep the cruiser's eye sensors tuned to look for Space Station Scardia," Trioculus ordered.

"Very well, sir," Commodore Zuggs replied.

Space Station Scardia was the cube-shaped distant outpost in the Null Zone where the Prophets of the Dark Side lived. At that very moment, inside the huge cube, Supreme Prophet Kadann awaited Trioculus's arrival.

Wearing his glittering, flowing prophet's robe, the black-bearded dwarf strolled slowly through one of Scardia's many corridors, on his way to the Chamber of Dark Visions. He was calmly sipping his tea, boiling tea that would have scalded the tongue of any ordinary man.

Kadann's tea was made from fungus-infested bark that came from the forest moon of Endor, where the furry Ewoks lived. Some said that it helped him dream of the future.

But Kadann's prophecies didn't always come from

dreams. The inspiration for Kadann's prophecies more often came from his secret network of very ruthless and efficient spies. They dutifully brought him secret information. This outpost was, for all intents and purposes, the Imperial Bureau of Investigation.

Information from spies helped Kadann figure out what was likely to happen. And if his prophecies didn't come true by themselves, then Kadann and the other Prophets of the Dark Side used their great influence to *make* them come true, using bribery, sabotage, and treachery—and sometimes even murder. In that way they kept their power and influence in the Empire.

When Trioculus and Grand Moff Hissa landed inside Space Station Scardia, they were met by a welcoming committee of Prophets of the Dark Side, including other dwarfs like Kadann, all the way up to High Prophet Jedgar, who was seven feet tall. The things they all seemed to have in common were their beards and gleaming black robes.

"Trioculus, Grand Moff Hissa, I trust that our worthy visitors suffered no ill effects from gamma radiation when you reached the Null Zone," High Prophet Jedgar inquired in a soothing voice. Jedgar always played the role of gracious host whenever anyone arrived at Space Station Scardia.

"There were no problems at all," Grand Moff Hissa replied. "Our ship is properly insulated from every form of radiation, including gamma rays."

The three eyes of Trioculus were greeted by the dazzling glitter of archaeological treasures gathered from all over the galaxy. Kadann's vast collection of

stolen valuables decorated every room and corridor of the space station, all arrayed in beautiful display cases.

"Is it true that Kadann has been collecting rare artifacts his entire life?" Grand Moff Hissa asked.

"Quite so," High Prophet Jedgar replied. "The baubles and trinkets in these display cases were gathered over a long span of years indeed."

High Prophet Jedgar turned and led Trioculus and Grand Moff Hissa to the Chamber of Dark Visions, where Kadann would receive them.

There they found Kadann up on a podium, seated on his ornate prophet's chair. Even with the podium, Kadann was so short he still didn't come up as high as Trioculus's chin.

At Kadann's side was a low table with many small balls resting on it. The balls seemed to be made of chalk, and each one was a different color.

"Dark Greetings, Slavelord Trioculus," Kadann said.

"Dreamer of Dark Dreams, Supreme Prophet of the Empire," Grand Moff Hissa began, "Trioculus is no longer merely the Chief Slavelord of the spice mines of Kessel. The Central Committee of Grand Moffs recognizes the mighty Trioculus as the Empire's one true leader—our new Emperor."

"And what does the mighty Trioculus want of me?" Kadann asked, though he already knew the answer.

"I've come to ask you for your dark blessing," Trioculus said. "As you once gave your dark blessing to my father, Emperor Palpatine."

Kadann picked up a yellow ball and held it in front of him. He closed his eyes and crushed the ball, which turned to powder in his hands.

Trioculus put his lips close to Grand Moff Hissa's ear. "Yellow is the color of a lie," Trioculus said. "What have I said that he doesn't believe?"

"That you are Emperor Palpatine's son," Hissa whispered. "Kadann knows the truth."

"Emperor Palpatine's son does not look like you," Kadann declared boldly.

Trioculus placed his hands carefully on his hips. "You call yourself Supreme Prophet of the Dark Side, Kadann, and yet you don't know that the Emperor fathered a son who was born with three eyes?"

"Since you ask, I shall tell you exactly what I know," Kadann said, in a forceful voice that showed not even a hint of fear. "The Emperor had a son he rejected from the day that son was born—a son he sensed might grow to become even more powerful in the Dark Side than he himself. And so he banished his son to the planet Kessel, where he was forced to work in the spice mines like a common slave." Kadann stared at Trioculus and smiled slyly. "Yes, his son was born with three eyes. In that you are correct."

Trioculus nodded with satisfaction.

"But where were those three eyes?" Kadann asked. "One was here." Kadann pointed to his own right eye with his forefinger. "And one eye was here." He slowly moved his forefinger to his left eye. Then Kadann moved his finger behind his head. "And his third eye was here, at the *back* of his head. With his third eye, he could see his enemies from behind."

Trioculus, whose three eyes were all at the front of his face, scowled.

"And you were one of those enemies, Trioculus," Kadann added. "As Chief Slavelord, you had authority over him."

Kadann picked up the red ball and crushed it in his hands. A breeze gusted through the chamber and blew the red-colored chalk onto Trioculus's clothes, staining them like blood.

"You seem to be accusing me of being a murderer," Trioculus said in a quiet but furious voice.

"Are you not?" Kadann replied in a very low voice. "Do you deny murdering Triclops, the Imperial royal son?"

Trioculus hissed beneath his breath and clenched his gloved right hand.

"Your Lordship, I beg you, remain calm," Grand Moff Hissa whispered to Trioculus. "Kadann knows many things. Whatever happens, don't become angry, or you will fail the test."

Trioculus gnashed his teeth and squeezed both of his hands into tight fists.

"The truth," whispered Grand Moff Hissa very quietly. "You *must* tell him the absolute truth. I promise, Kadann will understand."

"I may be a murderer," Trioculus said to Kadann, "but I never killed Emperor Palpatine's son."

"Are you saying that someone else killed him?" Kadann asked with a cagey smile.

"Obviously your spies haven't done their job, Kadann," Trioculus said, frowning. "They are telling you lies and misinformation. Perhaps Triclops would be better off if he were dead, but for the moment, he is still alive."

Grand Moff Hissa interrupted. "It was the secret judgment of the Central Committee of Grand Moffs that Triclops, the Emperor's son, was both mad and criminally insane. He was a menace to everyone he ever met, friend and foe alike."

"A very unfortunate situation," Kadann agreed, nodding his head.

"After Emperor Palpatine died in the explosion of the Death Star, those of us grand moffs who knew of the Emperor's wishes *had* to do something to protect what was left of the Empire," Grand Moff Hissa continued. "Did we dare let his son Triclops lead us—a son he had banished?  Why if Triclops were ever put in command, I have no doubt that he would have destroyed us all—every grand moff, grand admiral . . . and every Prophet of the Dark Side! In fact, we grand moffs believe that if ever Triclops is allowed to sit on his father's throne, he'll destroy the galaxy, planet by planet, until there is nothing remaining."

The black-bearded dwarf said nothing. He sat on his prophet's chair silently, stroking his beard.

"So you see, Kadann, we were in desperate need of a new leader," Hissa went on. "We couldn't keep fighting among ourselves, warlord against warlord. The lower-ranking officers and common stormtroopers knew there were rumors that a three-eyed son existed who had a legal right to his father's throne. And so—"

"So you decided your new leader had to be a man with three eyes," Kadann said, completing Grand Moff Hissa's sentence. "Someone the grand moffs thought they could trust. One who could claim to be the Emperor's son without arousing any suspicions."

"Exactly!" Grand Moff Hissa said, breathing a sigh of relief. "That's why we asked Trioculus, Slavelord of Kessel, to claim to be Emperor Palpatine's son and to serve as our new Imperial leader. Trioculus understands full well that the Central Committee of Grand Moffs is the *real* power behind the throne."

"I have fulfilled your prophecy, Kadann," Trioculus said in a confident voice. "You foretold that the next Emperor would wear the glove of Darth Vader. And as you can see, I wear it."

Trioculus held out his right hand, thrusting the glove of Darth Vader toward Kadann.

"If you have any doubts that this is the glove of Darth Vader," Trioculus said, "then see for yourself."

Kadann touched the glove and inspected it closely. "I recognize it," he said.

"So then you are satisfied that Trioculus has fulfilled your prophecy about the next Imperial ruler?" Hissa asked.

"He has indeed. The man who wears the glove of Darth Vader shall be our Emperor." Kadann then picked up the silver ball and spoke again. "But there is another prophecy about the one who wears the glove—" Kadann stopped himself in midsentence and fell silent.

"What is it?" Trioculus insisted.

Kadann squeezed the silver ball of chalk until it crumbled to dust. "Silver is the symbol of a Jedi Prince. There is a Jedi Prince from the Lost City of the Jedi who can destroy you."

Trioculus sneered in disbelief. "The Lost City of the Jedi is only a legend!"

"A legend only to those who don't know the truth. For it does exist. And you, Emperor Trioculus, must find the Jedi Prince who lives there, or you will not rule for much longer." Kadann now raised his right hand and pointed his forefinger upward, as though uttering a commandment. "This is your destiny. Find the Jedi Prince and destroy him—or he will destroy you!"

Trioculus frowned in dismay.

"And where *is* this Lost City of the Jedi?" Grand Moff Hissa asked.

"There are four continents on the fourth moon of Yavin," Kadann replied. "The Lost City is on the largest continent, deep beneath the ground, under the rain forest. Look for a round wall made of green marble in the forest. There you will find the entrance to the city. But you must find it soon. Very soon."

"I shall," Trioculus said, putting his hands on his hips triumphantly. "Not only shall I destroy the Jedi Prince, but as ruler of the Empire, I shall rid the galaxy of Luke Skywalker and the entire Rebel Alliance."

"Well spoken, Emperor Trioculus." And with that Kadann leaned forward and kissed the glove Trioculus wore. "You have my dark blessing," he said.

Trioculus smiled. It was one of the first real smiles of his life. However, it was cut short by a stabbing pain in the center of his head. Everything then became blurry and dim. Emperor Trioculus could see only dull blobs of light, shadows, and streaks of gray—and nothing more.

# CHAPTER 5
## A Path of Fire

Trioculus remained still, blinking his three eyes. Within moments his vision came back to him and he could see clearly once again. Following on the heels of Grand Moff Hissa, he departed from the Chamber of Dark Visions. He acted as if nothing happened. It was a perfect act. He didn't tell anyone—not even his trusted droid, Emdee.

A short while later, as Trioculus stood in the control room of his Imperial strike cruiser and looked out at the vastness of space, his thoughts were millions of miles away. He was thinking about Yavin Four and its vast rain forests. "How can I find the Lost City of the Jedi?" he wondered aloud.

"Someone on Yavin Four *must* know where the Lost City is," Grand Moff Hissa said. "The question is, who?"

"Perhaps Luke Skywalker or SPIN knows," replied Trioculus in an icy voice.

"Yes, SPIN, of course," said Grand Moff Hissa, referring to the Senate's Planetary Intelligence Network. His eyebrows shot upward as he suddenly got an idea. "I think you should send those Rebels an ultimatum— a warning so terrible that they won't be able to ignore it."

* * *

A few days later on Yavin Four, where the next meeting of SPIN was about to take place, Princess Leia and Han Solo were already seated in the conference room, waiting for Luke Skywalker. Han was so enjoying seeing Leia again that he'd put off his return to Bespin with Chewbacca.

"Han, I'm worried about Luke," Leia said. "He promised me he was going to show up on time for the SPIN meeting today."

"I'm worried too," Han said. "Have you noticed how strange he's been acting lately?"

"Luke *has* been acting different," Leia agreed. "The way he went off on his airspeeder the other day."

"Yeah," Han agreed. "Since when does he take mysterious journeys over the jungle, without any idea of where he's going?"

"He does things like that when he feels the pull of the Force," Princess Leia replied. "And now he's obsessed with finding a boy he says is from the Lost City of the Jedi."

"I think he's gone off the deep end," Han said with concern. "Luke never used to believe in the Lost City of the Jedi. He told me that because Obi-Wan and Yoda never mentioned it, then it must be only a legend. But suddenly he's convinced that it does exist—and he thinks the Force is going to lead him to it."

At that moment, Luke hurried in to join the other SPIN members in the Senate conference room. "Sorry I'm late," he said, out of breath.

"Same excuse as usual?" Leia asked.

"Afraid so," Luke admitted. "I was on my airspeeder again, searching for Ken. Still no luck."

The SPIN meeting started with a report by Rebel Alliance leader Mon Mothma on the problem of Imperial probe droids. "There's a new danger to SPIN," she explained. "Several enemy probe droids have recently penetrated Yavin Four's Air Defense Network. They've been spotted hovering over the jungle, as if searching for something. But their purpose is still unknown."

*EEEE-AAAAA-EEEEE-AAAAA . . .*

An alarm siren sounded in the Senate. Security had been violated.

*KCHOOOOING! KCHOOOOING!*

In the SPIN conference room the sound of laser blasts could be heard coming from the big defensive laser cannons on the domed roof of the building.

*BRACHOOOOM!*

The laser cannons must have missed their target, because something crashed right through the roof. Luke looked up to see a very small, perfectly round, black Imperial device flying under its own power. It zoomed around the SPIN conference room like a tossed ball.

Then it hovered in front of everyone.

Han Solo raised his blaster and fired once . . . twice . . .

But the black Imperial device kept dodging his blasts with short, sudden movements, continuing to hover in midair.

From inside his Imperial strike cruiser orbiting

Yavin Four, Trioculus watched what was taking place. The floating device was transmitting the scene inside the Senate, and Trioculus could see it on a screen from inside his navigation room.

He saw every SPIN member in the conference room. Above all he saw Luke Skywalker join Han Solo, in the attempt to destroy the floating Imperial probe device.

Then Trioculus saw the face of Princess Leia.

"That face . . ." he said to Grand Moff Hissa. "That woman . . ."

"Princess Leia," the grand moff confirmed.

"A first-degree renegade and troublemaker," Trioculus said, nodding.

"Darth Vader blew up her home planet of Alderaan, so he could teach her the importance of cooperating with the Empire," Grand Moff Hissa commented. "But she never learned."

"She has a striking face," said Trioculus. "Strong features, but soft. Not at all unattractive, considering that she's a Rebel Alliance woman with only two eyes."

"She's very dangerous," Grand Moff Hissa continued. "She murdered Jabba the Hutt. *Choked* him to death with the chain that kept her prisoner."

"I never liked Jabba the Hutt," Trioculus said. "A disgusting, fat slug—and a common gangster."

The spherical device was programmed by remote control, automatically dodging the weapons that were firing at it. As Trioculus watched the screen, he saw Luke Skywalker returning his blaster to his holster and drawing his lightsaber. Skywalker, the Jedi Knight whom Trioculus had vowed to destroy, would finally die at last, in just a few moments . . . that is, unless Luke Skywalker knew where the Lost City of the Jedi could be found and was prepared to reveal the information at once. Then Trioculus would see fit to spare Skywalker's life, at least for the time being.

As Skywalker tried to strike the sphere with his blazing lightsaber, it continued to jump away. Then it projected a hologram.

The members of SPIN watched in astonishment as the image of Trioculus appeared before them.

"Attention, Luke Skywalker and members of SPIN," the image of Trioculus said, "if by any chance you deluded yourselves into thinking that I perished back on Calamari, I'm sorry to have to disappoint you. I've just sent you a little gift that has penetrated your weak security system—this Imperial Antisecurity

Device. It is armed with an explosive of awesome power. In just twenty seconds I shall detonate it and destroy the entire Rebel Alliance Senate. However, to show my good will, I hereby agree to spare your lives if one of you announces at once the location of the entrance to the Lost City of the Jedi. The twenty seconds now begins. One . . . two . . ."

By remote control, Trioculus deactivated the hologram projector inside the device. From far away in space he was still able to watch the scene inside the SPIN conference room—a scene of desperate attempts to destroy the floating black sphere.

"I doubt we'll get any information out of them," Grand Moff Hissa said. "It's obvious they're more interested in fighting than in talking."

"Commodore Zuggs, activate the heat mechanism in the Antisecurity Device," Trioculus ordered. "It will require ten seconds to reach detonation temperature."

"Heat mechanism activated, sir," Zuggs stated, wiping a thin line of sweat that was flowing from the top of his clean-shaven head.

The view on the screen turned bright red as the device began to overheat. Five seconds to zero . . . four seconds to zero . . .

At two seconds to zero Luke's Jedi powers served him well. Directing his intense concentration at the black sphere, he forced it to stop darting back and forth in midair so it was no longer a moving target. As it remained steady and still, Luke sliced it in two with his lightsaber.

*KECHUNKKK!*

The detonator was in shambles, unable to trigger the explosion.

Out in space, inside Trioculus's strike cruiser, the Imperial ruler scowled when he saw that his first plan for finding the Lost City of the Jedi had failed.

"Proceed to Plan Number Two," Trioculus said. "The search and destroy mission!"

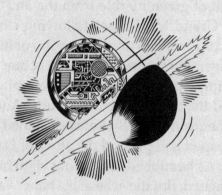

The sky over the rain forest turned deep purple with the onset of twilight. However, the beautiful sky was the last thing on Trioculus's mind as he landed on Yavin Four with a large fleet of escort carriers. The escort carriers were filled with enough TNTs to carry out his Plan Number Two.

TNT was short for Treaded Neutron Torch—a treaded, tanklike vehicle that could torch the rain forest by shooting neutron fireballs. TNTs could ride right through the most intense, blazing fire, without any harm to the stormtroopers riding inside.

As soon as Trioculus gave the order, the TNTs began to go into action over a wide area.

They started to torch the rain forest on the biggest continent of Yavin Four, shooting neutron fireballs everywhere. The TNTs filled the air with fire and smoke, and began to turn the forest into a heap of ash and charred timber!

"When the rain forests have all been destroyed, we'll find the entrance to the Lost City easily," Grand Moff Hissa explained. "We'll be able to locate the round wall of green marble from the air."

With Grand Moff Hissa following close behind him, Trioculus walked down the ramp of his Imperial strike cruiser. He wanted to see the action firsthand.

Looking around, he stared at the orange glow of flames and the billowing black clouds. And then the roar of a neutron fireball almost deafened him.

He gasped and pressed the glove of Darth Vader to his face. As he rubbed his eyes his right hand inside the glove ached. But the ache of his hand was the least of his worries.

When Trioculus opened his eyes he was now totally blind. He could no longer see even a dim haze or shadowy flicker of light. This was a darkness as pitch-black as a starless region of deep space.

The droid, Emdee, examined the new Emperor's eyes in the seclusion of Trioculus's private cabin on board his spaceship. He was unable to find any sign that Trioculus's eyes had been scorched by the fire or damaged in any way. Emdee confessed that this case was beyond his medical knowledge.

"Figure out what's wrong with my eyes, Emdee," Trioculus said, gritting his teeth. "Or I will have you

taken apart and sold for scrap metal!"

"My Emperor," Grand Moff Hissa interrupted, "we have just received a report from a team of stormtroopers. Near one of the jungle pyramids they spotted an alien—a Ho'Din, to be precise. Almost all Ho'Din know how to work medical miracles using plants and herbs. They're a race of healers, your Excellency!"

"Then tell them to capture that Ho'Din," Trioculus said, pressing his gloved hand against his eyes. "He shall figure out how to restore my sight— or I shall have *him* blinded as well, so he too can share my fate!"

# CHAPTER 6
## A Healer's Secret

Ken risked Dee-Jay's wrath to come Topworld again. And this time he not only gave Dee-Jay the slip, he ducked away from HC and Chip, too, by convincing both droids to help him with the library research for his latest homework assignment.

The assignment was to write a report on five major planets that had been wiped out by asteroids in the last half million years. HC and Chip were still probably deep in the Jedi Library, walking up and down the aisles trying to find out where the file on destroyed planets had been misplaced, unaware that Ken had hidden it under his bed in his dome-house.

Retracing his steps from his last trip Topworld, Ken soon spied Baji in the forest. The smell of smoke was in the air. And the distant forest fire was approaching.

Ken had never seen a forest fire before, except in holograms and pictures in the Jedi Library. His heart skipped a beat as he watched in horror. So much beauty was being destroyed in the fiery orange glow.

Ken cautiously approached Baji, not wanting to be seen. But perhaps the Ho'Din healer would know where Ken had left his computer notebook. Ken was determined to find it before the droids found out that he had lost it.

"Excuse me, sir," Ken said. "I met you once before, the day Luke Skywalker was here. Do you remember me?"

Baji jumped back, taken by surprise and somewhat startled. He smiled, nodded, and then without saying a word, he hurriedly collected more plants as fast as he could.

"I didn't mean to scare you," Ken continued. "I was just wondering, did you happen to come across my computer notebook? I think I dropped it somewhere around here."

Baji put a hand on Ken's shoulder and said:

> "Find it I did
>   In my hut it is hid
> Come there with me
>   And your notebook you shall see."

Picking up a sack that had flowers, plant stems, roots, and seeds, Baji led Ken to his thatch hut.

The little hut was bare. Baji had only a bed of soft leaves and a simple table and chairs. However, everywhere he looked, Ken saw that the hut was piled high with bottles containing seedling plants. All the bottles and jars were labeled in a language Ken couldn't read.

Baji kneeled to pick up Ken's computer notebook.

"Thanks, Baji," Ken said. "It was nice of you to

save this for me. And the droid who corrects my homework, HC, will sure be happy it's not lost. HC would really give me a hard time if I told him I'd lost it."

Baji peered through the open door of his hut and looked out at the red glow of flames far away in the forest. He shook his head sadly and frowned. Then he sighed and glanced down, looking away.

Ken stared at the reddish glow shining through the thick forest. There was no doubt about it, the fire was getting closer.

"I know what you're thinking," Ken said. "If the fire reaches your hut, then all your rare plants will be destroyed."

Baji nodded.

"I wonder how the fire started," Ken said.

And the reply was:

> *"The weapons of the Empire*
> *Did cause this big fire*
> *So now the end is near*
> *For a forest so dear."*

"Come home with me," Ken said. "You'd be safer there, underground."

Baji shook his head no.

> *"My work here is done*
> *From this forest I shall run*
> *My people are on their way*
> *A spaceship comes next day."*

"I can see that you'll be sorry to leave," Ken said. "It's a shame we haven't had the time to get to know one another, but I understand. Your home is on another world."

Baji nodded and smiled.

"I've got to be going," Ken said, "before the fire gets any closer. May the Force be with you, Baji."

Ken waved good-bye and started walking back in the direction of the green marble wall, where the tubular transport would take him back to the Lost City of the Jedi right away. Ken wanted to return before HC or Chip or Dee-Jay noticed that he was gone.

Ken glanced back to wave to Baji one more time. Suddenly Ken's heart thumped wildly. Three Imperial stormtroopers were approaching Baji's hut!

What was he going to do? Ken's first impulse was to dash toward them and shout, but he knew better than that. He was sadly outnumbered. And he had no way to defend himself or Baji.

Ken ducked, concealing himself in the foliage. He saw the stormtroopers point their blasters at Baji, capture the helpless Ho'Din healer, and lead him away.

Each of Baji's two hearts was beating rapidly as the stormtroopers forced him up the ramp of Trioculus's Imperial strike cruiser. His warm green blood became hot from fear as they led him past the maze of equipment in the control room, and into the private cabin of Emperor Trioculus.

The room was so dimly lit it was hard for Baji to

see the face of the Emperor, who was seated on an ornate chair. Grand Moff Hissa smiled politely at Baji, and Emdee stared at Baji as if he were a curiosity.

"At last the Ho'Din is here," Grand Moff Hissa said to the new Emperor.

Trioculus slowly leaned forward. Baji could see the Imperial ruler's three half-opened eyes. His eyes looked glassy, and the pupils were clouded.

"Ho'Din, if you ever breathe a word of what I'm about to tell you, you'll never live to see another Yavin Four sunset," Grand Moff Hissa said. "Tell me, are you a healer, like the rest of your people?"

Baji nodded but didn't speak.

"I command you to answer!" Trioculus shouted in a hoarse voice.

Suddenly realizing that Trioculus was unable to see, Baji replied:

> *"For the sick and weak do I care*
> *Be they powerful or meek, old or fair."*

"They tell me you're a Ho'Din," Trioculus said, "but at the moment, I can't tell. My eyes have betrayed me. I order you to heal me!"

"This is the most powerful patient you've ever had, Ho'Din," Grand Moff Hissa explained. "He commands the Empire. He is the ruler of the galaxy. Your life is in his hands."

Baji leaned forward and stared cautiously at Trioculus's glazed eyeballs. Then he noticed the glove Trioculus was wearing on his right hand. Baji kneeled down and touched it. Quickly Trioculus pulled his hand away.

"I asked you to examine my eyes, Ho'Din, not the glove of Darth Vader," Trioculus said. "Now heal me, understand?"

Baji replied:

> *"The glove you wear*
> *    Brings blindness and gloom*
> *Remove it now*
> *    For it seals your doom."*

"This glove *has* doomed many men, Ho'Din," Trioculus said, sneering. "Men who have angered me. But it will never doom *me*."

Baji replied:

> *"Since Darth Vader's glove*
> *    You now do wear*
> *Blind you are*
> *    And next goes your hair*
>
> *Take off the glove*
> *    Or there is no doubt*
> *Your teeth and nails*
> *    Shall all fall out*
>
> *Your hands will rot*
> *    Your face will welt*
> *Loud you shall scream*
> *    As in terror you melt."*

"I should have your eyes plucked out for saying that!" Trioculus exclaimed.

"Master," said Emdee, "the Ho'Din makes a medical point—one that did occur to me. The devices I inserted into the glove's fingertips so that you could send out deadly sound waves might possibly be the cause of your side effects."

"Go on, Emdee," Trioculus said, gritting his teeth, "continue."

"The sonic charges in the devices are probably causing damage to your nerve endings, affecting the optic nerves in your eyes."

"Perhaps you *should* consider taking off the glove, my Dark Lordship," Grand Moff Hissa said. "It's worth a try."

Reluctantly, Trioculus removed the glove of Darth Vader. Grand Moff Hissa and Baji couldn't help but gasp when they saw Trioculus's right hand—it was all red, blistered, and withered. And just as Baji had warned, the flesh on his hand had already begun to rot.

Trioculus blinked. The yellow, glassy look slowly faded from his eyes. "I can almost make out the shape of your face, Ho'Din," Trioculus said in a hoarse, deep voice.

"Your Excellency!" Grand Moff Hissa said. "The Ho'Din healer has brought back your eyesight!"

Baji reached into his pocket and took out a few kibo seeds—all that he had. He placed them in Trioculus's raw and withered hand. Then said:

> *"Eat the seeds of the purple flower*
> *Or your sight shall lose its power*
> *To be fully cured you must feed*
> *For a hundred days upon the kibo seed."*

Trioculus chewed and swallowed the kibo seeds. Moments later, his face brightened and his eyes cleared. A faint smile formed at the corners of his lips as his vision was slowly restored.

"Ho'Din, your medicine is impressive," Trioculus said. "I now see better than ever. Tell me, where can I get enough kibo seeds to eat them for a hundred days?"

Baji sadly lowered his head.

> *"Kibo flowers, so very rare*
> *Will soon be found nowhere*
> *For the flames that you have spread*
> *Shall soon make all kibo plants dead."*

"What is he saying, Hissa?" asked Trioculus. "I can't follow all of this Ho'Din's rhyming!"

"If I understand him correctly," the grand moff replied, "the kibo flower is very rare—nearly extinct. And your decision to burn the rain forests is about to destroy the last of them. You must eat their seeds for a hundred days, or—"

"Go on!" Trioculus said. "Then what?"

Emdee finished the sentence for the grand moff, who was too frightened to say any more. "Then, Master, you will go blind once again," Emdee said. "This time probably forever."

Once more Baji spoke:

> *"In my hut I have seeds in store*
> *Enough for all your needs and more*
> *But my hut soon shall burn*
> *Tell me, why does the Empire never learn?"*

Panicked, Trioculus ordered Baji to lead them back to his hut at once. The fire Trioculus had caused was about to destroy the last of the rare plants that were the only cure for his blindness!

Quickly they walked down the ramp of the Imperial strike cruiser and climbed aboard a mobile jungle transport vehicle. Baji gave directions. As they neared his hut, the flames were rapidly approaching, threatening to destroy the entire area.

Trioculus got out of the vehicle and hurried on foot toward Baji's hut. Suddenly one of the dozens of TNTs came roaring through the forest on its fast moving treads, firing its neutron torches.

"No, stop!" Trioculus shouted, as it aimed its front gun right at Baji's hut. "Stop, I command you!"

But the stormtroopers inside the TNT couldn't hear the Emperor. The TNT fired again, and Baji's dry, thatch hut started crackling as it burned.

A very desperate Trioculus went running into the fiery hut to save the kibo plants and seeds. But as he clutched them in his hands and tried to escape the hut, the doorway was blocked by a wall of flame.

# CHAPTER 7
# The Secret Code of Obi-Wan Kenobi

"If the fires in the rain forest are not contained," Princess Leia said to the members of SPIN, "then this moon of Yavin will face disaster. The rain forests are the source of our oxygen essential for the air we breathe. And thousands of medicines used throughout the galaxy are made from the rare species of plants that can only be found in these forests. There has been an invasion by a ruthless mutant—a three-eyed slavelord named Trioculus who calls himself the new Imperial Emperor. He is destroying our forests because he is on some insane mission to find the entrance to the Lost City of the Jedi. This evil madman must be stopped!"

With those words, the Rebel Alliance sprang into action. While Alliance fire fighters tried to put out the raging forest blaze, the *Millennium Falcon,* with Luke Skywalker, Han Solo, and Chewbacca aboard, searched for Trioculus's jungle base.

"I should be putting the finishing touches on my sky house right now, but instead, I'm stuck piloting the *Falcon* on another crazy mission for the Alliance,"

Han complained.

Not far behind them was a group of Alliance Y-wing starfighters. Their job: To destroy Trioculus's encampment and spaceships, giving the tyrannical dictator no hope of escape from Yavin Four.

The *Millenium Falcon* soared over the path of the spreading fire and followed it to its source. Soon Luke Skywalker located a clearing. Trioculus had taken over a Bantha grazing pasture that had been cut out of the jungle. His Imperial strike cruiser was on the ground, surrounded by a group of Imperial escort carriers. The tread marks of dozens of TNTs led away from the escort carriers in all directions.

"There's his base!" Luke said, communicating with the pilots of the Y-wings. "Go to it!"

As the Y-wings started destroying the grounded Imperial spaceships, the *Millennium Falcon* fired well-aimed laserblasts at a group of TNTs, taking them out one at a time.

The TNTs didn't just sit around waiting to be destroyed. They started firing back a barrage of neutron fireballs, blasting away at the low-flying *Millennium Falcon.* Han and Chewie had no choice but to guide the *Falcon* to an emergency landing in the forest below.

It was the worst landing of Han's career. The *Falcon* was unstable and shaking. It ripped through a maze of tall trees and thick vines, bouncing and sliding as it cut a gouge in the forest floor. "Arrrrroowgh!" Chewie moaned, knowing that the *Falcon* was now in desperate need of repair.

"Tough break, Chewie," Han agreed after the ship came to a stop. "The *Falcon*'s in trouble."

Luke, Han, and Chewie made a quick exit from their spaceship. The scent of smoke was everywhere, and they could hear the explosions of neutron fireballs in the distance.

"What do you think, Han?" Luke asked. "Do you figure the *Falcon* will ever be able to make the trip again from here to the Bespin system in eighteen standard time parts?"

Suddenly Han Solo saw a gleam of white in the corner of his eye. He glanced toward the object and drew his blaster. "A stormtrooper!"

Han fired a couple of times. Chewbacca hurried

over to see what the trouble was.

Luke propped himself up so he could see. "Stop, Han! That's not a stormtrooper! It's a droid I met. His name is Dee-Jay, and he's from the Lost City of the Jedi!"

"It's a droid named what from where?" Han asked.

Dee-Jay came toward them. Ken was alongside him, carrying his computer notebook.

"Commander Skywalker," Dee-Jay said. "You see what a disobedient boy I have here. No matter how many times I tell him not to come Topworld, he keeps coming back!"

"I had to find my computer notebook," Ken said. "I didn't know there'd be a fire, and TNTs, and storm-

troopers, and—" Ken suddenly glanced at Han. He recognized him from pictures he'd seen in the Jedi Library. "Wow, you're Han Solo, right?" He then looked over at the Wookiee. "And—you're Chewbacca!"

"Groooowwfff!" Chewie said, confirming that Ken had gotten his name right.

"We know who *we* are, kid," Han said. "What we don't know is who *you* are and what you're doing here."

"I'm Ken," he replied. "And I've always wanted to meet you, Mr. Solo, for just about my entire life. You're one of the best Corellian pilots in the whole galaxy!"

"What do you mean *one of*?" Han replied. "You know anybody better?"

"Snoke Loroan made the trip from here to the Bespin system in fifteen standard time parts," Ken said, without even batting an eyelash. "The best the *Millennium Falcon* has ever done is eighteen standard time parts. I looked that up in the Jedi Library."

Han rolled his eyes in amazement. Who *was* this kid?

"Okay, okay, I'll admit I'm impressed," Han said. "But Snoke Loroan got wiped out in the battle of Endor. We're talking about *living* Corellian pilots."

"Then I guess you're the best," Ken admitted with a smile.

"You've got that right," Han said and beamed. "Now I'll tell you what, Chewie and I have flown from one end of this galaxy to the other in the *Millennium Falcon*. If you or your droid know any way we can escape from this blazing firepit, we'll give you a free ride to the planet of your choice, someday." Han thought about his offer again. "Well, almost any planet. Kessel and Hoth are off-limits."

"You've got a deal!" Ken said. "That is, if it's okay with Dee-Jay."

"Commander Skywalker," Dee-Jay said, "the flames approach. You and your friends must follow me to safety. With your help, I may be able to stop these fires."

To Luke's astonishment, without walking very far through the forest, they arrived at the circular stone wall made of green marble.

"It's just like in my dream!" Luke said. "We're at the entrance to the Lost City of the Jedi!"

"My Corellian buddies will never believe this!" Han Solo said.

Dee-Jay led them through the opening in the wall. There they saw the circular tubular transport. As Dee-Jay approached, the door slid open, and they all went inside.

"Hold on tight," Dee-Jay warned. "You may find this ride a bit disagreeable."

The tubular transport dropped so fast, Luke and his friends felt as if they'd left their stomachs behind. They plunged through an underground region in total darkness. They kept dropping at an incredible speed, and soon they saw flashes of flickering lights from luminescent rocks.

At last they came to a stop at the bottom of the shaft, several miles underground. Luke stepped out and looked

around in awe. Here it was, the place he had been searching for. And in this illuminated cavern, it still seemed as bright and new as it must have looked when the first Jedi Knights built it a long time ago.

Luke tried to take in everything at once. The many dome-houses where the Jedi Knights used to live, the platforms filled with equipment of an advanced technology, and the transport vehicles and roads made of perfectly cut stone.

Dee-Jay led them past a huge building with a sign that read: Jedi Library.

"Those of you who live on the surface of Yavin Four think the weather of this moon is the work of nature," Dee-Jay said. "But it's not. It's actually controlled from down here, from our Weather and Climate Command Center."

They entered the Climate Command building. There Dee-Jay took them down a long corridor, as droids hurried by them busily from both directions.

"Thousands of years ago," Dee-Jay continued, "Yavin Four was a cold and barren world. The Jedi Masters who built the Lost City discovered that they could change its climate. All they had to do was find a way for the heat from the core of this moon to reach the surface.

"And so," Dee-Jay explained, "they cut many deep shafts into this moon, like the shaft of the tubular transport. The other shafts are designed for releasing steam and heat into the atmosphere. Using their weather and climate control system, the Jedi Knights made this moon grow warm and tropical. They even seeded its continents, so lush rain forests would grow."

Dee-Jay now led them into a gigantic room that had a huge machine the size of a planetary power generator.

"This moon is on a cycle—a six-month dry season followed by a six-month rainy season," Dee-Jay said. "The rainy season is due to start in several weeks. But if we could discover the code to speed up the weather cycle, we could start the rainy season now."

"That would sure douse the fires in a hurry," Han commented. "And none too soon. I won't be a happy man if the *Millennium Falcon* goes up in smoke."

Dee-Jay opened a control box. "We've got to figure out the code," he said. "I've searched nearly every file in the Jedi Library, but I just can't seem to find it."

"I had a dream," Luke said. "A vision of Obi-Wan Kenobi. He told me . . ."

Luke tried to remember what Obi-Wan Kenobi had told him in his dream. *Memorize this code*, Obi-Wan had said. *Its importance shall soon become clear to you.*

But what was the code Obi-Wan had told him to memorize? Try as he might, Luke couldn't recall it.

Luke took a deep breath and then exhaled. He let all his thoughts flow out with his breath. Then, as he inhaled, he felt the power of the Force pouring into him, filling him with energy and power.

Suddenly it was there: JE-99-DI-88-FOR-00-CE.

"I remember the code!" Luke exclaimed. "Obi-Wan didn't tell me what it was for, but I sure hope it activates the weather cycle."

Luke punched in the code. And it worked!

A screen in the room lit up and showed them what was happening on the surface of Yavin Four. Steam vents opened at locations all over the Yavin moon. The vents forced warm, moist air into the atmosphere. And with astonishing speed, storm clouds began to form everywhere across the sky.

Watching the screen, they could see the rain begin to fall. Then there was lightning. A torrential storm sent sheets of water pouring down from the black clouds. Soon the rain began to put out the fires in the forest.

In the torrential rainstorm, Trioculus, Grand Moff Hissa, and Emdee made their way back to what was left of their Imperial base camp. Reluctantly Baji accompanied them. To his sorrow, with a blaster pointed at his head, he was drafted into the Imperial army to become a staff physician.

As they surveyed the scene of the destruction, Trioculus clutched his jar of kibo seeds and touched his withered right hand to his face. It was no longer the same handsome three-eyed face he'd had before.

In Trioculus's rush to get the kibo seeds from Baji's hut, his face had been horribly burned. Now his face was covered with welts and blisters, and his skin was scorched.

Trioculus recoiled in shock at seeing that his Imperial strike cruiser had been blasted apart. And every Imperial escort carrier had either been damaged or exploded.

All that is, but one. In their push to achieve victory, the Rebel Alliance had neglected to destroy a single escort carrier.

The glove of Darth Vader, which Trioculus had left in his Imperial strike cruiser, was now lying in the mud on the ground. The rain lashed at Trioculus as he knelt to pick it up.

He didn't put it back on, but he kept it.

"You're going to make me another glove, Emdee," he said. "One that looks just like the glove of Darth Vader. No one must know that I no longer wear the real glove!"

"It's regretful that we didn't find the Lost City of the Jedi, my Emperor," Grand Moff Hissa said. "But if we send enough spies to Yavin Four, they'll keep looking for it until they find it—and perhaps they'll find the Jedi Prince as well."

"SPIN must be destroyed for this attack,"

Trioculus said. "SPIN—and every member of the Rebel Alliance in their Senate! Except . . ."

"Except whom, Lord Trioculus?" Grand Moff Hissa asked reluctantly.

"We'll take Princess Leia alive," Trioculus replied firmly.

And then they climbed aboard the remaining escort carrier. Once inside, they activated the power and took off, leaving Yavin Four behind. Trioculus then laid his head back in his chair and closed his eyes.

With his face painfully burned, and his right hand crippled and withered, Trioculus escaped into a dream, a dream of the beautiful Princess Leia. He could see her striking face, her strong but soft features. And he dreamed of making her his queen—the Queen of the Empire!

The time had come for Ken to bid farewell to the Lost City of the Jedi, and to HC and Dee-Jay, the droids who had raised him with devotion. Chip was to remain with Ken, to help him when he went Topworld to join Luke Skywalker and become the youngest member of the Rebel Alliance.

Dee-Jay had always known that the day would arrive when he would have to allow Ken to leave the Lost City and go off into the galaxy to live his own life. However, he had expected to wait until Ken was at least twenty, not twelve.

But Dee-Jay understood that the time was right for Ken to depart. From now on, Luke would give Ken guidance and instruction in the ways of the Force.

It was Ken's destiny.

Zeebo jumped into Ken's arms and licked his face, just like he had every single day, for years.

"I'm going to miss all you droids," Ken said. He thought about what he'd just said, and realized that he would probably even miss HC-100 every once in a while. "And I'll miss the Jedi Library," he continued, "and my dome-house, and I'll certainly miss you, Zeebo. Life won't be the same not having a mooka to wake me up every morning. But just think— I'm off to see the galaxy. My adventures with the Alliance have just begun!"

Luke hoped Ken would always remain enthusiastic, even after he learned more about the real world. And above all, Luke hoped that Ken would remain safe from the vengeance of the Empire. They may have stopped Trioculus from finding the Lost City of the Jedi, but Luke knew the cruel Imperial ruler would never rest until he got even—with each and every one of them!

**To find out more about Ken and Luke Skywalker and how they meet up with Jabba the Hutt's father, don't miss *Zorba the Hutt's Revenge*, book three of our continuing Star Wars adventures.**

# Here's a preview:

Zorba the Hutt entered the Mos Eisley Cantina and cleared his throat. All eyes turned to look at his huge, wrinkled body, with its braided white hair and white beard. They stared at his enormous reptilian eyes and his lipless mouth that spread from one side of his face to the other.

"I am Zorba the Hutt! Father of Jabba! Someone tell me where I can find my son!"

An awkward hush settled over the noisy cantina.

"I was told that Hutts are no longer permitted in Jabba's palace!" Zorba exclaimed. "Who owns my son's palace, if not Jabba?"

A green-skinned bounty hunter named Tibor, who was wearing a coat of armor over his reptilian skin, took a big gulp of his drink. "If I were you, Zorba," he said, "I'd calm down. Have yourself a drink of zoochberry juice."

"I will not calm down!" Zorba screamed. "I want information about Jabba! And I'll pay five gemstones to anyone who talks!"

The offer suddenly turned everyone in the cantina into an authority on Jabba. A dozen voices began blurting out all sorts of information at once.

But there was one voice that stood out above all the others. "You seem to be about the only creature this side of the Dune Sea who doesn't know that Jabba the Hutt is dead," Grand Moff Hissa said.

Zorba clutched his chest. "Dead?" Was his heart going to explode? "My son . . . *dead*?"

Zorba let out a wheezing sigh of grief that vibrated the whole room. "How did Jabba die?" he demanded.

"He was murdered by Princess Leia," a Jenet said, scratching the white fuzz that covered his body.

"Yes, it was Leia!" an Aqualish alien agreed.

"She killed him in cold blood!" Tibor shouted, pounding his body armor with a green fist.

"Princess Leia was Jabba's slave," the Twi'lek alien explained. "She had a chain attached to her. And she took the chain like this . . ." The Twi'lek twisted his own tentacle about his neck, to demonstrate. "And she squeezed the breath out of Jabba. It happened in his sail barge at the Great Pit of Carkoon."

Zorba's yellow eyes bulged from their sockets. "In the name of the ancient conqueror, Kossak the Hutt, I swear that this Princess Leia shall die!"

The bounty hunters murmured and exchanged approving glances. Then Zorba stared at Grand Moff Hissa. "Tell me, Grand Moff. Who is living in my son's palace?"

"Unfortunately, Jabba didn't leave a will," Grand Moff Hissa explained, "so naturally the Planetary Government of Tatooine took custody of his property—with the permission of the Empire, of course. At the moment, the palace is in ruins. Only the Ranats live there now."

"Ranats!" Zorba spit on the cantina floor in disgust. "I want ten bounty hunters!" Zorba announced. "Ten strong hunters to come with me to Jabba's palace! I will pay seven gemstones each!"

There were more than ten volunteers.

Zorba gave a belly laugh, a laugh so deep and loud one might have thought he was watching a prisoner being dropped into a vat of carbonite.

"A-HAW-HAW-HAWWWW!"

**Will Ken be tricked into revealing how much he knows about the Empire's darkest secrets? And can he survive being captured by Zorba the Hutt? Find out in *Zorba the Hutt's Revenge*, coming soon.**

# Glossary

**Baji**
A Ho'Din alien, a healer and medicine man who lives in the rain forest on the fourth moon of Yavin. Baji is wise, peaceful, and speaks in rhyme. He collects plants, rare stems, roots, leaves, and vines that are good for making medicines and that he fears may become extinct. He then tranports them to his home planet of Moltok, for other botanists to study.

**Chip (short for Microchip)**
Chip is Ken's personal droid. His outer metal is silver. He is the size of a twelve-year-old boy and is programmed to look after Ken. As much as he tries, more often than not he is unable to talk Ken out of doing adventurous things.

**Commodore Zuggs**
A bald, beady-eyed Imperial officer who pilots Trioculus's Imperial strike cruiser spaceship.

**Dee-Jay (DJ-88)**
A powerful caretaker droid and teacher in the Lost City of the Jedi. He is white, with eyes like rubies. His face is distinguished, with a metal beard. He is like a father to Ken, having raised him from the time the young Jedi was a small child.

**HC-100 (Homework Correction Droid-100)**
His appearance resembles See-Threepio, though he is silver in color, with blue eyes and a round mouth. HC-100

was designed by Dee-Jay for the purpose of correcting and grading Ken's homework. He walks in perfect step like a soldier on the march, and talks like a drill sergeant. He frequently pops into Ken's dome-house without any warning for surprise homework checks.

## Ho'Din

Gentle, ecologically aware aliens from the planet Moltok who have snakelike tresses growing on their heads. They are primarily botanists and prefer nature to technology. Baji is a Ho'Din healer. Ho'Din natural medicine is recognized throughout the galaxy.

## Jedi Library

A great library in the Lost City of the Jedi. The Jedi Library has records that date back thousands of years. Most of its records are in files in the Jedi master computer. Others are on ancient manuscripts and old, yellowed books. Gathered in this library is all the knowledge of all civilizations and the history of all planets and moons that have intelligent life-forms.

## Kadann

A black-bearded dwarf, Kadann is the Supreme Prophet of the Dark Side. The Prophets of the Dark Side are a group of Imperials who, while posing as being very mystical, are actually a sort of Imperial Bureau of Investigation with its own network of spies.

Leaders of the Empire seek Kadann's dark blessing to make their rule legitimate.

Kadann made the prophecy that the next Emperor would wear the glove of Darth Vader. Kadann's prophecies are mysterious four-line, nonrhyming verses. They are carefully studied by the Rebel Alliance for clues about what the Empire might be planning.

## Ken

Ken's existence has been kept a secret, and so has the location of the Lost City of the Jedi, the city in which he is growing up. His origins are mysterious and his parents are unknown to him. For some reason the droids of the Lost City have decided not to reveal this information to him until he is older. Ken has been given the impression that he may be a Jedi Prince. He doesn't know the significance of the birthstone he wears around his neck on a silver chain.

When Ken was a baby an unknown Jedi Knight in a brown robe took him to the Lost City and left him there for safekeeping. The chief caretaker droid of the Lost City, Dee-Jay was instructed to raise Ken and educate him.

Ken has certain Jedi abilities that have come to him naturally, such as the ability to cloud minds, to mind-read, and even the power to move small objects by concentrating on them.

Ken goes to school in the Jedi Library in the Lost City, where he is the only student. There he is taught by Dee-Jay. Ken is not permitted by the caretaker droids to visit the surface of Yavin Four until he is old enough to defend himself against evil.

## Kibo flower

A type of very rare purple flower Baji collects. The seed from the kibo flower can restore sight to the blind.

## Lost City of the Jedi

An ancient, technologically advanced city built long ago by early Jedi Knights. The city is deep underground on the fourth moon of Yavin. The entrance is marked by a seven-foot wall of green marble in the shape of a circle. Inside the circle is a tubular transport that descends to the Lost City.

All the greatest secrets of the Jedi are recorded in the Lost City, stored within the master computer of the Jedi Library. For ages, droids have been in charge of taking care of the city. The only human there is twelve-year-old Ken. However, Ken does have a pet—a mooka named Zeebo.

The existence of the Lost City has long been one of the Jedi's greatest secrets. Though Kadann knows it exists, neither he nor any other Imperial knows its location.

## Moltok
The planet where the Ho'Din live. It is where Baji comes from and where he has his greenhouse.

## Prophets of the Dark Side
A sort of Imperial Bureau of Investigation run by black-bearded prophets with their own network of spies. The prophets have much power within the Empire. To retain their control, they make sure their prophecies come true—even if it takes force, bribery, or murder.

## Space Station Scardia
A cube-shaped space station where the Prophets of the Dark Side live.

## TNTs
TNTs, or Treaded Neutron Torches, are tanklike vehicles that shoot fireballs. They were originally designed for use in the spice mines of Kessel, blasting into rock to open up new mine shafts. However, they work just as well as jungle vehicles, plowing their way through rain forests.

## Topworld

An expression that refers to the surface of the fourth moon of Yavin. When the droids of the Lost City of the Jedi talk about going Topworld, they mean taking the tubular transport to the surface.

## Triclops

Though Triclops doesn't appear in this book, we have learned that he is the true son of the evil Emperor Palpatine. Triclops is a three-eyed mutant, with one eye in the back of his head.

He is shrouded in mystery. All that is known about him for certain is that the Empire considers him insane and fears disaster if he ever were to become Emperor. For some mysterious reason they still keep him alive, imprisoned in an Imperial insane asylum and a secret Imperial reprogramming institute.

The Empire has always denied Triclops's existence, keeping him hidden away as a dark secret. But there have been so many rumors about the Emperor's three-eyed son that to put an end to the whispers and gossip, three-eyed Trioculus falsely announces he's really Emperor Palpatine's son and the new ruler of the Empire.

The rumors, however, still persist.

## Zeebo

Ken's four-eared alien pet mooka, he has both fur and feathers.

# About the Authors

**PAUL DAVIDS** and **HOLLACE DAVIDS** met by chance in Harvard Square in 1971, just after Paul saw George Lucas's first movie, *THX 1138.* It was love at first sight. Paul had graduated from Princeton and Hollace from Goucher and from the master's program in counseling at Boston University. But they discovered that they had grown up just a few miles apart in Bethesda and Silver Spring, Maryland. They married several months after they first met.

Paul, who began making 8mm science fiction movies when he was ten, studied writing and directing at the American Film Institute in L.A., and a few years later became a member of the Writers Guild (WGA), writing for Cornel Wilde and (with Hollace) George Pal, a pioneer of movie science fiction. After teaching children with learning disabilities, Hollace became the FILMEX Society Coordinator for the L.A. International Film Exposition.

In 1977, the year *Star Wars* premiered, their daughter Jordan was born. In 1980, the year *The Empire Strikes Back* opened, their son Scott was born, and Hollace began coordinating all the major film premieres and parties for Columbia Pictures. And when *Return of the Jedi* opened in 1983, Paul's accomplishments included writing *She Dances Alone,* a movie starring Bud Cort and Max von Sydow, and producing for the TV show *Lie Detector*. He then worked as production coordinator for about one hundred episodes of *The Transformers*, some of which he wrote. Currently Paul is an executive producer of a movie for HBO based on the book *UFO Crash at Roswell*, and Hollace is vice president of publicity and special events for TriStar Pictures.

Paul and Hollace published their first book in 1986, *The Fires of Pele*, a fantasy about Mark Twain in Hawaii. Now they are hard at work on even more Star Wars books for young readers.

# About the Illustrators

**KARL KESEL** was born in 1959 and raised in the small town of Victor, New York. He started reading comic books at the age of ten, while traveling cross-country with his family, and decided soon after that he wanted to become a cartoonist. By the age of twenty-five, he landed a full-time job as an illustrator for DC Comics, working on such titles as *Superman*, *World's Finest*, *Newsboy Legion*, and *Hawk and Dove*, which he also cowrote. He was also one of the artists on *The Terminator* and *Indiana Jones* miniseries for Dark Horse Comics. Mr. Kesel lives and works with his wife, Barbara, in Milwaukie, Oregon.

**DREW STRUZAN** is a teacher, lecturer, and one of the most influential forces working in commercial art today. His strong visual sense and recognizable style have produced lasting pieces of art for advertising, the recording industry, and motion pictures. His paintings include the album covers for *Alice Cooper's Greatest Hits* and *Welcome to My Nightmare*, which was recently voted one of the one hundred classic album covers of all time by *Rolling Stone* magazine. He has also created the movie posters for Star Wars, *E.T. The Extra-Terrestrial*, the Back to the Future series, the Indiana Jones series, *An American Tale*, and *Hook*. Mr. Struzan lives and works in the California valley with his wife Cheryle. Their son, Christian, is continuing in the family tradition, working as an art director and illustrator.

# T·H·E
# LUCASFILM
## F·A·N C·L·U·B

NEW

# WHAT NEW ADVENTURES ARE COMING FROM LUCASFILM?

The answer to this question and more can be found by joining The Official Lucasfilm Fan Club! Membership entitles you to a one-year subscription to the quarterly Lucasfilm Magazine! Each issue features exclusive interviews, and beautiful full-color photos, with the cast and crews of the latest Lucasfilm productions such as the *Young Indiana Jones Chronicles* as well as past productions such as *Star Wars* and *Raiders of the Lost Ark*. In addition, you'll find informative articles on the special effects projects at Industrial Light & Magic, the latest in computer entertainment from Lucasfilm Games and more! Plus you'll receive, with each issue, our exclusive Lucasfilm Merchandise Catalog filled with all the latest and hard-to-find collectibles from *Star Wars* to *The Young Indiana Jones Chronicles* including special offers for fan club members only!

If you love the kind of entertainment only Lucasfilm can create, then The Lucasfilm Fan Club is definitely for YOU! But a one-year subscription to The Lucasfilm Fan Club Magazine is not all you receive! Join now, for only $9.95, and we'll have delivered right to your front door our brand new, exclusive *Young Indiana Jones Chronicles* Membership Kit which includes:

- • Full-color poster of 16 year-old Indy, Sean Patrick Flanery!
- • Full-color poster of 9 year-old Indy, Corey Carrier!
- • *Young Indiana Jones Chronicles* Sticker!
- • *Young Indiana Jones Chronicles* Patch!
- • Welcome Letter from George Lucas!
- • Lucasfilm Fan Club Membership Card!

AND MORE!

Don't miss this opportunity to be a part of the adventure and excitement that Lucasfilm creates! Join The Lucasfilm Fan Club today!

---

**YES, SIGN ME UP FOR THE ADVENTURE! I WANT TO JOIN THE LUCASFILM FAN CLUB!**

Enclosed is a check or money order for $_____

U.S. DOLLARS ONLY; 1 YEAR MEMBERSHIP— (9.95 US) ($12.00 CANADA) ($21.95 FOREIGN)

Charge to my: ❑ Visa ❑ MasterCard

Account # _____

Signature _____

Name (please print) _____

Address _____

City/State/Zip/Country _____

Send check, money order or MC/VISA order to:
**The Lucasfilm Fan Club**
P.O. BOX 111000
AURORA, COLORADO 80042 USA
© & TM 1992 Lucasfilm Ltd.

**JOIN FOR ONLY $9.95**

SK52-7/92